The Fault Lines Founding Liberty

The Fault Lines Founding Liberty

Sarah Bacaller

RESOURCE *Publications* · Eugene, Oregon

THE FAULT LINES FOUNDING LIBERTY

Resource Publications
An Imprint of Wipf and Stock Publishers
199 W. 8th Ave., Suite 3
Eugene, OR 97401

www.wipfandstock.com

PAPERBACK ISBN: 978-1-7252-7824-0
HARDCOVER ISBN: 978-1-7252-7825-7
EBOOK ISBN: 978-1-7252-7826-4

Manufactured in the U.S.A.   09/03/20

Prelude

Just enough resistance to register difference,
subtle, quiet; gentleness effective.
Firm yet still, with quietly beckoning gesture,
focuses in; gives space for my own
evaluation, thought, response.
Not like force that pushes past,
asserts dominance and pushes hard,
as if so much must be resisted, when really
there is nothing much—
a wisp, a fleeting thought, a moving other.
Force sees a frightening monster, but
the more force used,
the more force needed so,
numb, silent, empty grows ever-escalating violence . . .
Not like your gentle definition, validating reception;
you step aside, receive, accept,
with just enough resistance to register difference.
This gives me space to think, feel, hear, move, respond,
but never quite to pin you down;
I am invited to hear the echoes of you,
and to learn.

Chapter 1

SHE WALKS IN WITH understated sureness, granddaughter's hand in hers. Her soft grey hair sits atop straight shoulders in a loose bun. I am scoping out my companions for the next hour. The children have ballet and the adults have a musty room. Thankfully I have a small crawling human to occupy me, which provides an excuse to avoid adult interaction. Meanwhile, I listen.

Conversation develops slowly between those in the room; my attention is drawn by the comments of the grey-haired woman. These are not mundane; they are thoughtful and include observations on politics, people, events. She takes an interest in others. This makes *her* interesting. I feel bored with myself in comparison, and lonely. Her gentle certainty makes me feel I am missing something.

And so it goes, one week after another. She speaks with clarity yet not with intrusion. I observe hungrily—what *is* it that she's got? I glean tidbits from what I hear and over time, begin participating in polite chats peppered with baby-related distractions.

Thursdays are now a mildly interesting possibility amongst tiring, long weeks of hard work and interrupted sleep.

* * *

A ballet concert wraps this rhythm up and the curtains of another year are drawn, with tutus and tiaras and excessive photographs. A year of here-and-there conversations exit my Thursday stage, and the sting of loss surprises me. This has become something, yet its significance has grown so gradually that I only perceive its weight once I lose it. There is more I want to know. The grey-haired woman's words have woven loose threads, beckoning to be taken up and followed . . .

I have this random idea that perhaps I could help gather her life stories into a book . . . for her, or for her family, or maybe for others. This book is the first thing I've felt excited about in ages; it gives energy and hope . . . but the idea deflates as soon as I remember that it's near impossible to get even ten minutes alone to shower at the moment. Yet I can't quite give this up, because it feels good to have a spark and tragic to lose it. So I file her away for a rainy day, perhaps a day when leaving home alone again feels possible. With a skerrick of hope, I ask for her phone number as we part for the last time. It is strange to think that after a year of weekly crossings, I may never see her again—just like that.

"It's been nice to get to know you," I say. She smiles, skeptically perhaps; am I misreading her? Maybe I don't really know her at all.

She gives me her phone number, and I suddenly feel like the fool I am. I don't even know her name. I store her number in my address book as "Casey's Grandma." By the time I should have known and didn't, it was too embarrassing to ask. So I went along, pretending I knew more than I did.

* * *

My hand shakes as I dial the number. Two years have passed. My daughter has started school, my son sleeps slightly more than he used to. On the walk to school one morning, my daughter and I reminisce together about ballet classes and I remember the grey-haired lady. I decide to champion her cause and help collate stories of her life into a book, even just for her family—whoever they are.

So I dial her number while quaking absurdly, goodness knows why. Am I going to tell her about the book? Just say I want to catch up? Invite her to my place, or cross my fingers and hope she invites me to hers?

* * *

I knock on the door with a galloping heart and am let into a spacious, light-filled house; contemporary and comfortable. I wait nervously for my host to appear, remembering the quiet confidence that initially caught my attention.

I hear shuffling and she emerges around a corner . . . walking frame before her. I double take. She is bent, her shoulders hunched. I struggle to hide my shock and disorientation, searching almost anxiously for her posture of confidence. It has only been two years but where has she gone? She is not who I remember.

"I write, you know," she nods toward me. This is the first thing to leave her lips; not so much as a hello. She speaks with certainty and conviction, completely out of nowhere.

"Hello," I say, "I . . . I . . ." I falter violently, thoughts tripping over. She is silent and I am confused. Does she want me here? Am I intruding? *"I write, you know"* . . . the words replay in my mind. I am unsure and then more unsure. Those knobbly fingers, that wilted figure . . . Are they symptoms of a frail, wobbly mind? I try madly to make sense of it. She seems so adamant and I force myself to engage politely, asking "What do you like to . . ."

"Oh, everything," she says, cutting me off as she waves her hand and gives a slight head toss. It seems she is discarding any whiff of doubt I've cast in her direction; she is sharp enough to have read the end of my question too, and perhaps the questions behind it.

"I write everything. Children's stories, articles, poetry . . . especially now."

What am I to make of this? Does she recognize me? It seems hardly the same woman as two years ago. Or is it me who has changed, noticing things I didn't see before? It's a strange feeling, you know . . . When you fall into uncertainty regarding your conversation partner's sanity, it rather makes you doubt your own.

* * *

We are sitting at the dining table over peppermint tea.

"So you write?" I ask, deciding to take her seriously. "I don't recall you mentioning that." She just looks ahead.

I look at her, awash with uncertainty.

Then she looks at me. Can she read *me*?

"I can show you something I have written."

"Okay."

But she makes me wait. We talk a polite but stilted conversation for about ten minutes, until I run out of steam and politeness. I don't quite know why I'm here anymore. Just as I am about to leave, she hands me a slip of paper, folded.

"Read it when you get home. And do come again."

Will I? Truly, it has been a disaster for my career as a biographer.

* * *

Later that evening, I pull the crumpled paper from my purse. It is so small. What could it possibly say? She has old-lady handwriting, but it is not as wobbly as I expect. I read:

They met in a crowded room. He was lonely; she, hungry. It could have been something, but it wasn't. Yet it was all the more for that.

What am I to make of that?

"It was just odd," I tell my husband as we wash the dishes. "I've never known anyone to age so quickly."

He shrugs. "It's been a few years. Is she sick?"

"I don't know. At first, I didn't know if she remembered me. I *think* she did but I'm not sure. She seemed so much more . . . *direct*. Her cleaner let me in and then when *she* walked in, the first thing she said . . . the first thing! . . . was '*I write you know.*' It was rude!"

"She sounds a bit off kilter."

"That's what I thought. I was trying to work it out the whole time."

"Bet you're glad you went though."

"I don't know."

"Will you go back?"

"Dunno."

"I'm sure she appreciated the conversation."

"Maybe. Who knows?"

The dishes are done.

* * *

I admit to myself that I am intrigued by her slip of paper, just a little. Why such an enigmatic line? I turn it over mentally:

They met in a crowded room. He was lonely; she, hungry. It could have been something, but it wasn't. Yet it was all the more for that.

Is this somehow significant? A code to unlock? Is she trying to tell me something? How could something be *more* by *not* being? Truthfully, this unveils that old awareness in me; I am still bored, aimless. The thought of getting to know this woman's stories, the thought of storming into her life as some kind of romantic artist, gathering the threads of her life with my ink, pulling them into cohesive unity, has given me purpose. To present her as a heroine, and myself as a bold artist—the potential has been wonderful. But I realize my mind has been dazzled by a fantasy that is only shown for what it is in its dismembering. I have been misguided. She doesn't need me. And my project won't be what I, deep in the folds of my subconsciously lonely heart, have planned. I am annoyed, mostly because I am sick of discovering the twists and turns inside me—I just want to do something useful.

And so, I go back.

* * *

The second visit leaves no doubt as to her soundness of mind. She is all there, and more. Yet something *must* have happened. She is direct yet also withdrawn; her conversation is not socially conventional.

"Those ballet classes were two years ago. Casey must have grown a lot!" I say.

"Oh yes, indeed." She smiles and is silent.

"Do you see her much?"

"Mm-hmm."

Pause.

"Does she like school?"

"Yes, mostly I think. Thank you."

Pause.

"Which school does she go to?"

She doesn't seem to have heard. I sit quietly, not knowing what to do. Repeat my question? Invert it and tell her about my daughter?

"Do you ever take her to school?" I ask. *Can she drive?* I wonder silently.

The clock ticks.

My ideas are running out and so is the sweat on my palms. Is she going to ask about *my* daughter? That would be polite, but she seems entirely unaware. I volunteer the information.

"My daughter is in prep too."

"Yes."

Silence.

We sit there, sipping tea. It is uncomfortable and I force myself to endure it. I am simply tired of initiating conversation, and if she can hack silence, so can I. Last time, her parting words were, "*Do come again.*" She had sounded keen . . . why? Why, especially, if we are sitting here silently? It is so weird. My heart beats less steadily than the ticking clock as the silence wracks my nerves. Would it be rude to leave? I don't know why I'm here.

"I have more time on my hands now," I continue with effort, "So . . . I thought I'd get in touch with you again."

She nods, looking into her tea.

I falter. I want to ask how her last two years have been, to figure out why she's aged so much—but there's an invisible barrier, a sense of intrusion . . . and a strange fragility for a moment. If she wants to share something, maybe I should leave it to her. There is a sense of space, but I'm not sure whether it's coming from her or me. Her quietness highlights my gaps.

I sit a little longer and then check my watch. It hasn't even been twenty minutes, but I'm done. Plus, I feel ashamed of my stupid book idea. I realize her initial reaction when we met again after those intervening years was probably annoyance at my intrusion; I have been so misguided. She probably can't stand me; I, for one, am ready to forget all this . . . but I can't, because I am flogging myself for my idiocy and my overgrown propensity for mistakes. Such thoughts are constant; today they swirl while I fiddle with my scarf and avoid eye contact. I break out of them by making excuses about getting back to the kids.

But before I rush out the door, she shocks me again, because she invites me back.

My chronic fear of self-assertion leads me to politely acquiesce—another reason to flog my idiocy. I pretend to be busy and choose a date six weeks away. Who knows, perhaps my kids will be sick then and I'll be able to cancel.

* * *

Arms filled with fabric of varyingly musty scents; these are now piled into tired tubs cracked with constant use. I take the short trek to the machine that frees my days from washing and scrubbing, to set and forget . . . at least for an hour, before the hanging, the collecting, the folding, the putting away. *Does she still fold her own washing?* I wonder.

* * *

Mattock to dirt, thrust down with flagging vigor; the weeds run energetically, never chased down, never fully eliminated. Growth, productivity, life, abundance . . . this is what I seek . . . yet not for the weeds, which grow unbidden and most vigorous of all. I find little patches of time to shape and nurture life that seems so vulnerable, so easily eliminated—yet that can be hardy and resilient too. *How to facilitate the resilience and growth of that which will nourish?* I wonder. *Am I going round in circles?*

* * *

My knife swishes through onion, meeting the wooden board with a faltering rhythm; stinging scents rise and evoke unbidden tears. Oil heats in a pan, salt is sprinkled; there is vigorous sizzling as vegetables are added handful by handful. I stir, then rinse off piled dishes while dinner cooks, thinking meandering thoughts of varying veracity. *What is she eating for dinner?* I wonder.

I'm not sure that trust can be decided once and for all. There *is* a certain consciousness in trust—but intentionality cannot force it. As force increases, trust retreats like a frightened animal. Only I *can* make decisions to position myself in vulnerability; to take risks, more or less calculated, more or less terrifying.

Sometimes, my risks are poorly calculated and vulnerability is not worth the pain. Trust grows slowly, slowly, reinforced by countless expressions of reliability, of kindness. One hint of danger, one sniff of suspected maleficence, and my trust shrivels. I slide down the slippery snake back to square one. Every time, a reset. It is too exhausting. I am tired of it. How does trust become resilient?

Strangely, in my day-to-day rhythms, I am becoming used to the idea of her.

Chapter 2

SIX WEEKS HAVE PAST and nothing much has changed; nothing noticeable at least . . . I feel awkward about visiting the old lady yet intrigued by her invitation to return. At least I know what to do when I arrive now: enter the dining room, put down my bag, sit at the white table in the clean, open space. It sits adjacent to her kitchen, with a view of the patio through glass doors. Her shaking hands make me nervous as the tea is poured; her use of a teapot elicits a twinge of surprised pleasure in me.

I attempt pleasantries again, but somehow don't feel quite so obliged this time. She shuffles about, apparently organizing things for my comfort, and I sit and gaze around aimlessly, squirming because I don't know where to look. There's a nice dish of biscuits on the table and I'm tempted to shove three in my mouth at once (because when was the last time someone laid out a plate of biscuits for me?). Of course, I am restrained. My sense of propriety and self-consciousness combine to reign me in and I sit tight until she offers. She gingerly takes a seat and we sit with our tea. I am waiting for her and perhaps she is waiting for me. Who moves?

As I bring the tea to my lips, she pipes up:

"Do you believe in God?"

The question drops like an unholy stench between us.

"Ahhha . . . mm-hmm . . . huh-huh . . ." I splutter as my tea goes down the wrong way.

I can't breathe; is it the errant tea or the thunderbolt question?

I clear my throat, look up, and catch her gaze. My heart is beating fast, but I won't show a hint of it.

"Are you alright, dear?" she asks innocently.

"Ahem . . . yes, sorry . . . hm-hmmm . . . just went down the wrong way." I feign a smile, and somehow taste peppermint in my nose. Perhaps if I don't answer her original question, she'll forget it. She can't know what she's stumbled upon here, and I sure as heck won't let on. Silence reigns; it has worked.

The tea goes down rightly this time; it's soothing, like the silence. Funny how things change. Right now, I like silence.

"So?"

Damn.

I breathe deeply. She is staring at the ceiling, as if watching a fly. I can't see it.

Well, I reflect, *at least I'm not supplying all the questions this time. She isn't so scary, is she?* My oscillating mind figures I *could* perhaps tell her after all. If she doesn't like it, she won't invite me back.

"I don't like talking about God anymore," I say honestly, perhaps letting on more than I realize, "though it depends what you mean by God, I guess."

"Ah!" is all she says and something sharpens in her gaze, as though I have come into focus. I watch her, ready to bat off whatever comes next.

We're on the silence rollercoaster again. But she doesn't probe and there is space to consider, and to hear myself zinging between all the possible defensive stances or phrases I might need to employ.

"Are you still hungry, dear?"

I am in the mood for honesty now.

"Yes . . . always hungry," I say. "But the biscuits are good," I add, frightened of sounding ungrateful.

She looks at me quickly and gets up slowly, chair legs scraping the tiles, crooked fingers grasping the table's edge.

"Don't get up," I interject. "I'll help."

"I'm stronger than I look," she retorts. Then she pauses.

"Well . . . I'd like to think so." I hear a sigh, see her slump. "Yes, okay. There's a fruit bowl in the fridge and some cake in a container in a cupboard to the left of the dishwasher."

I oblige, but she still gets up and shuffles around with me, as though we are engaged in an odd dance, simultaneously and cooperatively avoiding intrusion into one another's space. She gets out plates, slowly, carefully, while I source the victuals and we resume our seats. I bring cake to my lips and nibble but now that it comes to it, I feel weird about eating, especially chewing; self-consciousness is hard to swallow . . . She is looking at me. I try not to notice. *Why* is she looking?

"Are you alright, dear?"

"Oh, um, yes. Fine thanks. Thanks for the cake."

She is still looking . . . observing. It makes me shy; I wish she wouldn't.

"I'm sorry if my question was too bold," she offers.

"No, no, it was fine," I say. It wasn't really fine. But I have come to terms with it.

"I was a little curious as to how you would respond."

"I choked on my tea!"

"Yes. I was also a little curious . . . *am* a little curious . . . about why you want to come . . . here, I mean."

"Well, I . . ." My grand literary visions died weeks ago and they don't attempt a revival, even as I am conscious of their denial. "I don't know. I mean, the last two times I came because you invited me, but the first time . . ."

Will I offend her? She nods slightly, so far unsurprised by what I've said. I venture forth and feel like I'm stepping off a precipice.

"I think I'm a bit lonely. And maybe bored." I cringe, as though waiting for a blow but she just nods again, as though she simply accepts my words at face value. It's odd; unexpected. I don't ask about that slip of paper yet.

Before I leave, she invites me back, again.

"Is it convenient for you to come again?" she asks.

"How about this time again in a fortnight?" I ask.

"Of course. Whatever suits you. I will look forward to it."

"Oh!" I say with some surprise, "Thanks!"

Yet on my way home, that pleasant moment recoils into its opposite. My stomach knots up as her "looking forward to it" feels like a burden, an expectation. What does she want from me? What if I can't give it?

I think I am also slightly disappointed she hasn't given me anything to read.

* * *

In a week, I receive a surprise. A letter in the post—from her! Needless to say, I am curious; needless to say, I then begin fearing she is needy and begin to asphyxiate—the obligatory recoil that seems always to exist. Tearing open the envelope reveals a simple note; a simple note on a single piece of notepaper saying, "Thank you," with her signature underneath. That doesn't feel needy. That feels . . . nice.

* * *

Her unexpected question is stirring something. It is awakening a beast in the depths of my consciousness. A dangerous beast, one best kept hidden; one I hoped would slumber into dissolution.

Only . . . its presence is a haunting specter and all the more because of the energy required to tiptoe round it, to keep it at bay. Unhappy memories arise; fears which I have been busy enough to occlude. Guilt pours over me as the many standards I fail to meet rise within my mind, tumbling over each other with their sheer volume and velocity, overwhelming me and making even tiny tasks occasions of painful indecision and trepidation. I have too many unanswered questions. With a grinding pain, I wish they would disappear.

I am distracted and elsewhere as I walk my daughter to school, manage my way through the day, ensure the ongoing life, health, and safety of my tempestuous son, and try to keep back the tide of squalor. *Why am I avoiding God?* I wonder as I sweep floors.

What am I afraid of? My parents had thought that regular church attendance whilst growing up would have a positive effect on my "moral development," but I've left that practice behind.

I shake my head, as voices and memories from the past take shape. Week upon week of lying in the aisle at my parents' feet, filling coloring books whilst the service dragged on and on . . . funnily enough, church became less boring the day I realized I could listen. Something switched. I realized there were things at stake, and I learnt very quickly—the lingo, the expectations, the routines. Eternal destiny began to matter. I absorbed more than my parents ever imagined I would. They were stuck with a religious zealot, who held up every move to strict religious scrutiny. Ironically and unfairly, my parents had given me a hard time about my passionate faith—it had been more than they'd bargained for.

Then as a young adult, I had proved myself one of those dreaded seeds cast amongst the thorns, strangled by the weeds of other concerns. Amidst study, marriage, raising kids . . . who had the energy to worry about eternal destiny? All the extra requirements lumped on top of "just getting by" were too much. I could not bear the endless, divinely ordained self-scrutiny; the feeling of having someone looking over my shoulder all the time.

But the nagging sense that I am a fallen prodigal lingers . . . and "God" hasn't gone away. Somehow, God has gotten under my skin; the questions are too deep to excise. Always looking over my shoulder, I am haunted by the specters of unanswered questions. My fear of unresolved judgment is nourished by insecurities, but I don't know how to uproot them; they have grown bigger than me. And who am I kidding? The self-scrutiny hasn't gone away. The harder I try to ignore God, the more frequently God turns up.

That's why I'd choked on my tea.

* * *

Like cold tentacles slipping round me from behind, the anxiety raised by the old woman's question grabs me, pulls me under. Submerged, tumbling, swirling through a torrent of anxiety, I can't sleep, can't breathe. Dammit, oh why, oh why did she ask me? *"I don't really care. I don't really care!!"* I scream inside. But that fear, that animation of death, has latched onto my heart like a grappling hook and I am bleeding, tearing at the seams. *"God!"* I scream inside, *"I don't believe in you!!"*

A horrible voice bubbles up from the depths and whispers its reply: *"Why are you telling me then?"*

What happens in the dark stays in the dark; it's another world. All is new when morning comes. Two parallel versions of myself: one pulled under; the other, head above water, coping normally with the tasks of every day.

* * *

The old woman sits with her husband in the sort of *comfortable* that might come after decades of shared existence—notwithstanding the complex tangle of threads that interweave their lives.

"How was the visit this afternoon? Did you have a nice time?" he asks.

"Oh yes, lovely," she replies. "Although . . ."

"Yes?"

"She seemed a bit perturbed when I asked about God."

"Dear! You shouldn't have."

"I was curious!"

"You're always curious. You'd think eighty years would have cured you of it."

"You know better than that."

"I do. What did she say?"

"She choked on her tea."

"Oh no. Have you frightened her off for good?" He half chuckles.

"I don't think so. I hope not. I'm . . ." she paused. "I'm not quite sure what she wants."

"What do you mean?"

"By coming. By visiting. I'm not sure what's she looking for."

"Well, maybe she doesn't know either. You're too suspicious."

"Not suspicious . . . curious."

"Well, you'll both figure it out as you go along. Ready for bed?"

"Yes. Thanks, love."

He helps her up and off they go.

* * *

Since the old lady has woken the beast by bringing up God, or since God has come to haunt me via the old lady, I have been asking myself if it is worth putting myself through this. I am un-settled and unhappy and the painful tension that her questions raise has fastened a permanent knot in my chest. When I try to think about it, my stomach drops. When I try to forget it, the knot tightens. I feel bound, unsure where to turn next. To leave it all behind? To run away? But I'll have the same questions and I'll have to face them eventually.

Maybe this is better than boredom.

I begin to wonder whether I might begin explaining it to her. No one else knows. Is this a sense of resolve gradually building?

Chapter 3

I FIGHT WITH MYSELF all the way to her place. I barely know the woman. Sure, we spent a year of Thursday mornings together, but who knows what she is like outside that time. Does she yell at her grandchildren? Does she keep her word? Is she judgmental?

For some reason, I am dead scared of all this. I tell myself that it doesn't matter, but there is this pull—almost a desperation to show myself, for someone to see what I am like and what I think, and to hear them say that I am despicable and damned. I am rebelliously driven to test myself against her to see if I get the only answer I feel I have ever heard, all my life. That I am not good enough. So, when I knock on her door, I am shaking again.

"I went to church for years," I blurt out as soon as I see her, before I can change my mind. It is the first thing I say. Now we're even. An odd greeting? One all. She nods, not unkindly, and that is all. I follow her meekly to the dining table in silence, having retracted speedily into my shell, like a snail that has been poked with a stick.

I don't know why I've brought it up. Why have I brought it up? Surely the peppermint tea and biscuits would have been fine on their own, without this pungent thematic intervention.

She pours the tea and doesn't choke when she drinks. *She* hasn't flinched.

Then, "How are your children?" she asks.

Well!

I cannot figure this woman out. Nevertheless, I welcome the distraction and fill her in on recent shenanigans: unplanned haircuts, rogue slime, belly button coloring in. She laughs, and I like it. We sit. The clock ticks. It is okay though I am not quite at home; I feel over-conscious of my body.

She seems different since our first cup of tea . . . or am I? Is it possible that *she* was shy initially? I think back to her comment, "*I write you know.*" I guess anxiety might lend discourse a piquant flavor when it oversteps shyness, especially mingled with passion or offense.

"Have you heard of Martin Luther?" she asks, out of nowhere.

"Ummmm . . . You mean the civil rights leader? *I have a dream*?" I reply, trying to get my bearings.

"No," she shakes her head.

"Oh." Whoops. Dumb.

"May I give you a task?"

I shrug and say, "Sure," curious as to what she's got in mind.

"Go home and look up Martin Luther. Do some research, then come back and tell me what you find."

"Okay," I agree, "I will." It gives me a good feeling, though I've no idea how it's relevant. Neither church nor God come up again.

* * *

Weaving through suburban streets back home, an odd sight strikes me. Two figures are moving violently, having an obvious altercation. As I drive closer, my car slows slightly but my heart speeds up. It's a man and a woman, and for all I can tell they are yelling in each other's faces, shoving . . . I pass but keep watching in my rearview mirror and see the guy throw a punch. What the hell? What am I meant to do?

I pull into the nearest side street and park the car, thinking madly. No one else seems to be around. I could drive back and park opposite, or drive past and honk the horn. Or pull up and ask if everything is okay.

"No, you can't!" I tell myself. Damn, it feels wrong. I sigh, feeling entirely impotent, guilty, and hateful, and drive the rest of the way home. I have failed the good Samaritan test.

I walk in the door, shaking a little, and am greeted by my son. "Hi Mummy!" he says. "Guess what? Grandpa came over!" I look quizzically at my husband.

"My Dad was here?" I ask as I unload my keys and bag. He nods.

"Oh! He didn't mention he was coming."

"He only came for ten minutes."

"Just to say hi?"

"Not quite."

"Huh? What for then?"

He looks tense.

"What's wrong?"

He sighs. "Your Mum and Dad are moving."

"Again?"

"Yeah. But further this time."

My stomach clenches with all the power it has left.

"Where?"

"The other side of the country."

"What! Why?"

"You won't believe this. Brace yourself. They feel like 'God' is leading them there."

My head spins and I feel like the floor is collapsing under me. Not *God* again. I cannot make sense of this.

"My *Dad* said that? But they don't go to church anymore. Why's he saying something like that?"

"I dunno. Probably to legitimize their decision."

Damn God! I wish the fool would leave me alone.

These blasphemous thoughts arise and I am ready to be smote, just to add to the emotional tumult.

"You don't think God *actually* told them to go?" I query. I don't think so, but it pays to be sure. Of course, if *God* has told them to go, I can hardly argue.

"You know my thoughts on that."

"Of course." It is reassuring. But then the next issue . . .

"Why the hell didn't he wait 'til I was home to tell us? Was he avoiding me?" It hurts to think it.

"I don't know. He popped in, gave the kids chocolate, had a quick chat and left."

My heart is struck and my head spins on top of everything else. I feel confused, rejected, and shocked. My parents have moved multiple times in the last ten years, but always within similar suburbs, and never longer than an hour's drive away.

"Do you think something's going on that they haven't mentioned?" I ask. "Are they hiding something? Maybe something health related or . . . or . . . relational?"

"What's relay-shnell?" asks my youngest, reminding me of his presence. He has been there the whole time.

"Good question Bub," I reply, lifting him up for a cuddle. "What *is* relational?"

* * *

I lie alone in bed and cry. My feelings are too knotty to hope for untangling. I can only surrender to their weight. Soon my head aches; nose breathing is impossible. And, I discover that I want to tell someone. I want to tell my little old lady.

* * *

I'm spinning in circles for days until I suddenly remember Martin Luther—*not* the guy with the "I have a dream" speech. I ignore the loads of laundry to fold and sit down at my computer.

Martin Luther.

I scan through various sources of information, reading and watching.

Sixteenth-century monk. Church reformer. Challenged the corruption of the church. Hmm, interesting. *Johann Tetzel, the selling of indulgences, and the Ninety-Five Theses.* Lots to learn. *Polemics on Jews.* Not so good.

Then I find an account of Luther's conversion experience. Well, not strictly a conversion experience it seems; he was already a monk and a biblical scholar, and in those days, who had a choice about religion anyhow?

But I read about a man who is wracked by guilt, tormented by his failings, and who feels damned. He is never good enough. He even admits that he *hates* God. I almost cry in relief at the solidarity.

One day, I learn, Martin Luther has a revelation: it is that faith alone justifies him before God . . . not good works, not anything he does. He is a saint and a sinner all at once, and it is fine. Somehow this realization sets him free, and it turns the old order of things upside down.

I read about this liberation with the same hunger that beset me when I first met with the understated sureness of the old lady. *How is it I've attended church for years and have heard nothing about this man?* I wonder. Then again, there are words here that have dug well-worn tracks in my mind over years of repetition: justification and faith, grace and salvation, righteousness and sin. But what do they really mean? What do they mean beyond the clichéd definitions I have learned to reel off? How do they *feel*? I recall the lessons of my childhood and youth, which have set down such deep roots that I am obviously still bound, despite appearances. *I am a sinner. Everything I do is corrupt, nothing is pure, as is the case for all of fallen humanity.* I wonder where and how Luther's ideas fit in with this?

* * *

"Why did you ask me to look up Martin Luther?" I ask the next time we sip tea.

She smiles gently, "Because you made an interesting comment when you arrived."

"Oh . . . you mean my church comment?" I screw up my face. She nods.

"Sorry about that," I say meekly.

"There's nothing to be sorry about." She is resolute.

"Oh!" Absorbing her pleasing response, I continue: "But what about Luther?"

"Well . . ." she begins, "I suppose that was my way of responding to your comment on church. I was trying to open up the topic without you feeling interrogated."

Her deftness and sensitivity lead me to appreciate the space I've been offered. I realize with surprise that she knows as little about me as I do about her; maybe less. What does it mean to know a person?

"So," she smiles, "what did you find out?"

"Well, Martin Luther was a sixteenth-century monk. He was very unsettled about his own sinfulness. And he had major problems with the church."

"Indeed."

"He went to Rome and got angry about the corruption there. The church had been selling indulgences to raise money for rebuilding St. Peter's Basilica and Luther didn't like that. He thought they were taking advantage of ordinary people."

"You've done your research!"

I smile and continue, "There's one thing I don't get."

"What's that?" she asks.

"People were told that if they bought indulgences, dead relatives would suffer less in purgatory. But I didn't find out what purgatory was."

"Purgatory is an idea found mostly in Catholicism," she replies. "I think it's an inbetween place where souls go after death and experience punishment for purification, before being sent to heaven."

"But . . . what's the point of salvation then?" I object, watching to gauge her reaction. Does she know what I'm talking about?

"Go on," she says, inviting me to keep going.

"Well, at the church I went to, I learned that . . . we're saved by believing in Jesus' death and resurrection, because he paid the price for our sins. We can go to heaven when we die . . . and not to hell, where we deserve."

She nodded ruefully. "That's what I was taught too."

"You know what I'm talking about?"

"More or less."

"Did you . . . do you . . . go to church?"

"It depends what you mean by church," she smiles, returning my response to her first God question. "But yes, I did," she continues. Aha. So, I wonder how much I can get away with saying. And I think back with embarrassment to my comment about not liking God. It reminds me of something.

"Hey, did you know Martin Luther felt like he hated God?" I announce it as evidence in my defense.

Yet, she doesn't thunder with disapproval. She nods and smiles.

"So," she says, "What do you think? Does Jesus' death pay the price for our sins? Does it save us from God's wrath?"

"Doesn't it?"

She shrugs and looks at me. "Punishment is an odd concept, don't you think? Does it make us better? Does it help us grow? Should fear motivate goodness?"

Silence.

"Punishment teaches right and wrong! We deserve it. We've fallen away from God's perfect intentions for humanity. There's a cost in that," I reply with sudden adamance; the me of fifteen years ago has been strangely summoned and begins to possess my perspective.

I am torn between expecting her hearty affirmation and her violent disagreement; for which should I prepare?

She simply nods quietly, accepting what I say. I am suddenly hesitant, unsure of my assertion. Her acceptance gives more reflective space than any reaction could . . . though I'm not sure she agrees with me. She doesn't seem to agree or disagree.

I excuse myself and go to the bathroom, more to give myself time to think than anything. When I come back, she has begun to crochet. It doesn't look so easy with those wonky fingers, but she persists.

"Shall we sit outside?" she asks.

I nod and we walk out the glass doors to the little deck, sur-rounded by lively green bushes and flowers hopefully turned to the sun. We sit and she continues to crochet, while I fiddle with a couple of lavender heads that I have mindlessly picked from a bush.

Outside is good. Outside is spacious. There is no pressing need for the exchange that four walls demand; we sit facing the same direction. She is busy with her work; I am busy fiddling and thinking, which go together. I spy a couple of weeds and lean down to pull them.

"Dear," she begins after a time. Her appellation doesn't go un-noticed, and I soften. She continues, "The gospel message of salva-tion . . . of being saved by grace through faith, as Luther reminds us . . . It's meant to be *good* news." She puts down her crochet and turns toward me, intensely focused. "But does it seem *good* to you?"

"Oh yeah!" I reply, adamant again; the softness disappears as quickly as it arrived. My defenses are up. "It's the best news!"

But I am an idiot. If this was what church was about, I'd still be there. I cannot explain why the hell I am defending a place I no longer belong to. But I feistily continue:

"Jesus' death shows how much love and grace God has even though we don't deserve it. And I don't have to worry about any-thing anymore. God's got everything in hand. That's why I'm a Christian," I finish with horrid duplicity, because if I am one, I'm the worst that exists.

She pulls right back, just nods with gentle acceptance and returns to her crochet. I am expecting a fight, and there is none. She is accepting, but I have a nagging uncertainty as to whether she agrees again.

No return question comes, but I imagine one. In my mind, she asks if it has worked. She asks if I am liberated from fear and worry; if my salvation has saved me, here and now. I could be half honest and say *no* and blame it on myself—I've fallen away; I don't trust God enough; my faith is weak and I don't do anything to nourish it. There are any number of possible permutations along these lines.

But a horrible tension begins to grow as I'm suddenly not so sure anymore. This internal purgatory is being brought into question by the gentle, certain dignity of this unfathomable woman. I begin to see the cracks in self-blame.

But I can't face the alternative. I just can't.

Besides, it is almost time to leave. Amongst all this, I haven't even mentioned my parents.

* * *

I lie in bed that night thinking it all over, especially my weird flip-flopping between positions, each one that I feel so adamant about but cannot sustain. What do I believe? Who am I? Where do I stand? I think of my parents, who are moving across the country, apparently at the will of God. I still want to tell my little old lady. I have the odd idea that I could write her a letter. So the next day, I do.

Chapter 4

I AM WALKING MY daughter home from school and the kids are dawdling to look at bugs and sticks when my phone rings. It is her. My heart speeds up as I answer. In calm, even tones she thanks me for my letter and for my trust. She asks when I would next like to come and see her. *Soon*, I say. *How about Friday?*

It is settled.

* * *

"What I don't understand is this," I tell her. "For years they took me to church, hoping it would shape my moral development. Then I imbibed it and invested in it, and *they* shied away from it. *They* stopped going and told me I was too serious! I did what they wanted and they weren't happy. Now that I've let it go, *they* dive in headfirst! It's a bloody comedy. I don't understand; it doesn't make sense."

My heart is on my sleeve but by now I am willing to wager she won't attack, and besides, I am driven by the absurdity of it to jump into risky exposure. I am by turns angry and despairing.

She doesn't pry. She's so quiet that it's almost like having a conversation with myself . . . only it's not. I am still trying to figure out if I like it or if it is plain odd . . . but at the moment, it's the best I've got and I run with it. I am free to say what I want, or not to say anything.

"I feel trapped; there is no way out—not from my parents, not from God. God keeps turning up to haunt me . . . in your questions, in my parent's weirdness, in my own thoughts."

"I don't mean to haunt you," she says.

"I know," I sigh. "It's my fault."

"No. You've got hanging questions. You're eager to know."

"Yes, but I'm also terrified of what I will find out, so I keep making false starts. It's *horrible* to think about God." I bang the table with my fist and shock myself with the sound of it.

"Yes," she says quietly, "I know."

"It sounds terrible, but . . ."—my feelings are avalanching now and I am caught in them, tumbling outside of myself—"sometimes I . . . I hate God! God feels like . . . death!"

I have spoken rashly again, but I have spoken truly. I almost shut my eyes for the sense of impending doom.

But she sits quietly. Clearly, doom is not on her radar. She is not disapproving, and this powerfully contests my otherwise looming sense that I am about to be smote.

"I've been there," she says. "Any thought you might have about God, I've probably had it too."

"You have?"

"Yes, of course. We're human, we're alive, we feel things. It's okay."

I don't understand. I am sure that any other person I know of serious Christian allegiance would jump down my throat, cursing my blasphemousness and calling me a lost cause; trying to control my perspective. Whatever God is, it is surely not as patient as this little lady. What does she think of my ideas and my outbursts? I can't tell specifically, but I know she doesn't mind. She isn't threatened—not by me, nor by my overwhelming feelings and existential yearnings. I want to throw my arms around her in total relief to have found someone who can accept me as I am, without the right answers, even if just momentarily. I don't, because I am way too self-conscious. But somehow, a constricting rope has been loosened. These questions that feel so taboo, these isolating wonderings and deadly realizations, are redeemed as moments of connection.

"It's just that being accepted by God seems to depend on so many things," I say, laying myself bare, "and there are so many ways to go wrong! Every step is like walking into a trap. I'm damned if I do and damned if I don't . . . literally!"

"Ah, forget about damnation!" she says with a smile and a wave of her hand.

We laugh and doom dissipates. Drinking in the absurdity, to laugh at myself is freedom.

"Seriously though," I resume, "I can't just say, 'God doesn't exist,' without feeling as though, somewhere out there, my name has been struck from the book of life. But when I tick the boxes, there are always more to tick! I don't deserve to go to heaven anyway. I'm a prodigal. But I sort of *want* to be one. How will I return home unless I've been given the freedom to leave? How will I know what I think about God unless I consider all the different possibilities?"

She raises her eyebrows and sits quietly.

"There a lot going on in your world," she observes.

"Oh. How do you mean?"

"Your parents. Managing your own family. Working through these questions. For example, parents shape who we feel we need to be for acceptance and approval."

"In church, they taught that we shouldn't seek any person's approval—only God's. If we have God's approval, we don't need to worry about what anyone thinks."

She nods.

"But that doesn't make any sense!" I continue. "I feel like such a failure because I want people's approval. My parents', my husband's, my friends'. I always used to tell myself that God's approval was all that mattered, but it never seemed to *do* anything. Nothing changed. My fate is sealed, I guess."

"Our conversation on Luther was interesting."

"What do you mean?" I suddenly remember my outburst and look down sheepishly. "Oh. Sorry."

"What are you sorry for?" she asks.

I look up. "I dunno. I was rude in that conversation, and defensive. You were exactly right, in everything you said. I don't feel liberated. No matter how much I hear about grace or salvation, it doesn't work. It doesn't sink in or make sense. I thought there was something wrong with me. I thought I was doing something wrong."

In the silence, my observations are like illuminated particles in the sunlight, dancing wildly but gently drawn by another force to settle softly on the ground.

"Dear," she says softly, "would you do me a favor? Would you run to my room and bring my cardigan from the bed?"

"Yes, of course," I say.

Her room is interesting. She has photos of people I assume are her children, her grandchildren, her husband. Her husband! I can't believe I haven't thought about this earlier. She's never said anything about him, and I've never met him. Why not? She hasn't said much about her children either. It is so strange that some people air the particulars of their lives upon first meeting, whereas others keep them tucked away. Is it something to be suspicious of? Or does it mean her treasures are held so dearly that they are shared only with those she trusts?

I walk back with her cardigan and even help her to put it on. It feels strange to touch her; she is more real than I thought. She is actually there. I feel so self-conscious and excuse myself, promising to come back in a fortnight.

Actually, I soon begin counting down—because I know exactly what I want to ask.

* * *

It is a stormy, windy day. Driving rain obscures my vision, but I arrive safely. It is not boring to repeat this rhythm. It is comforting, even though my heart still beats hard when I walk in the door. Life is a strange mix of contradictions. People who want it all black and white miss so much. My question burns within.

We sit in the lounge room today, she in a mustard colored recliner, me on the floor.

I soon begin to rifle through her bookshelf, thinking how nice it would be to curl up on the floor here and read.

"Borrow any book you like," she offers.

"Really?" I am pleased. "Thanks!" Her bookshelf is filled with literary giants—Shakespeare, Austen, Hugo, the Brontës—and plenty of unfamiliar but intriguing titles. I pull off the oldest looking book I can see; Dickens. I haven't read any Dickens before. I sit down and flick through; this copy was published in 1897. It is neat, but the distraction doesn't last; my question bubbles away in the background.

I can suppress it no longer.

"Do you ever pray?" There. I have asked.

"Pray?" she says, slightly surprised. She pauses. "It depends what you mean by 'pray.'"

I squint thinkingly.

"I guess I mean the usual. Directing thoughts or words to God."

She nods thoughtfully and says slowly, "I only pray by accident. Sometimes, a prayer jumps unplanned from my heart. Old habits die hard. Actually, I feel annoyed at myself for it, as though I'm reverting to begging."

She is so unorthodox.

"But . . ." I begin.

"I know." She shrugs. "I know," she says again, almost surrendering. "Apparently it's essential to faith. But it doesn't feel right." She gathers herself, "Now, just cue some righteous religious person to tell me that prayer is not about me, and to wag their finger at my lack of discipline. Trust me, I've heard it all. I really have. But I know myself; I've learned the hard way. Prayer is a cop out. Instead of begging someone else, I need to take responsibility for myself. Decide. Act. And face my vulnerability. Prayer is too safe, passive, and desperate for me." I am reminded of the dignity that first drew my attention to this woman. She is winning me over. She is strange and unpredictable, yet invites my trust.

"I just cannot presume to do it," she continues. "Plus," she winks, "they haven't realized yet that it doesn't actually work!"

She is a heretic! She is a heretic, and here I am feeling joyously free at her heretical observations! She is not afraid of being smote and I love it. Yet something in me wants to explore the consequences to their full extent.

"But, but . . ." I say, "what about your spiritual life?"

"What spiritual life?" she shrugs. "My life *is* my life."

This can't be right. I can't trust this after all. The pendulum swings and I am crowded in and under siege.

"But . . . prayer is the ultimate necessity of faith!" I argue. "Who in history would deny the importance of prayer to faith?" My duplicity is sickening—I yearn for the answer she is giving, and yet I fight it, hard. "Plus, prayer is self-developing. And people are thoroughly convinced that in praying they're having some kind of spiritual influence on things. *And*," I add, and the old zealous Christian in me swells with strength and fear, needing to tidy this mess up, as if summoned by magical words, "miracles *do* happen! You can watch clips of them on the internet! Crazy stuff. Healings, powerful effects, miracles."

She shakes her head slightly.

"What!" I say, more emotively than I have yet been. "Don't you believe me? Look, I can show you right now!" Why am I getting so riled up? Why does it matter? Why is this last bastion worth fighting for, when moments ago I was gloriously free? No sooner does freedom begin to glimmer over the edge of the horizon than I close my eyes and furiously fight it. She is the punching bag for my incessant recoil.

I want to find a video to show her. Explain that it is real.

But she goes quiet. She looks out the window. Why does she always do this? Sometimes I want a fight, but there is no fighting her. She withdraws, she makes space, and I am left stupidly throwing fists into midair.

She begins talking about the recent weather and her garden, as though the whole debacle of a conversation hasn't even happened; as though it hasn't ruffled her in the slightest. Really, the weather?

We don't return to the subject that day. It is swept away by time's tide. So is my zeal. Against her maturity, I feel tiny.

* * *

When I check the mail four days later, there is a letter from her. Fingers shaking slightly as I open the envelope, I recall my last visit with shame, and fear that she has written to give me the scolding I deserve. It reads thus:

When I was in my forties, I read a terrifying book. I was desperate to know about death and what happened afterward, to gain some kind of reassurance. My sister had just committed suicide. The book explored near-death experiences—or post-death experiences— where individuals either on the verge of, or exhibiting clinical death, somehow resumed their lives. Their stories, when they awoke, were of heaven, of untold horrors, of long-lost relatives encountered, of surveying one's life in the presence of Christ, of demons and terror. There was great variation, but always a story.

Reading the reports, I was confronted with the reality of life after death; of some kind of interpreting post-death consciousness; of evidence of the infinite, one way or another, and of our being entangled with it.

I reeled; existential vertigo ensued. I couldn't finish the book.

Why did I take it so seriously? Why couldn't I just write it off as pointless conjecture or unscientific rubbish?

We all have to die at some point. I could have tossed the issue aside, dismissed the book as manipulative trash —but wouldn't that have been evading the ultimate question? I had been taught that it was of absolute importance. I wanted a way through. And my own sister had just died. I was awash with grief and desperately vulnerable, addicted to spiritual experiences and desperately searching for truth. This was exacerbated by unfeeling monsters who called her suicide "sin."

Crisis is rather unhelpful for continued, steady existence amid responsibilities. My life had seemed full of crises up to that time. Were they self-inflicted? There were things in my life left unanswered. I couldn't rest. And perhaps that was my downfall. Death is not easily integrated or subsumed into life. Perhaps it cannot be. It is too much. So, if one cannot live with tension and irresolution, one will not get so far in life. I wanted things solved before I moved on, like neatly typing up one mathematics equation before moving to the next. Surety. I didn't want to continue with fault lines underneath me.

But what is the alternative choice? A life without fault lines is not possible . . . yet I couldn't seem to settle for it.

I look forward to seeing you again soon, dear. I enjoy your company.

The letter ends abruptly. I am left sitting in the unresolved tension she has just admitted to hating. She has taken me there with her. I hate talking about death; it makes me ill. I feel both angry and sorry for her . . . and her sister. She has shared something very personal. It is about time, because here I am, always feeling entirely transparent.

She seems different in her writing.

* * *

I don't want to bring up the letter because it means bringing up her sister, yet I can't ignore it. I have taken her up on last time's offer and have been immersed in Dickens for the last twenty minutes. The peace of her house is a relief; my mind rests without the clutter of chores and children's chaos, and it is almost other worldly. She is sitting at a small desk in the lounge room, writing a letter. I am lying on the floor, reading. I feel like a child who is relaxed in her parents' home, though it's not a feeling I know well.

Thoughts of her letter flit across my mind, distracting my reading, as I wonder how to broach it. I am certain of saying the wrong thing. Thankfully, I don't have to say anything. After half an hour, she finishes and turns to watch me. I become conscious of her gaze and sit up, still pretending to read but not at all able to concentrate because she is watching.

Half a minute later and she is still watching me. I wriggle uncomfortably. Smooth out my jumper. Fiddle with the tassels on my scarf. This is socially inappropriate. Darn old woman, why does she just sit there so quietly? Is she waiting for something? Waiting for me? For what?

"Ummm . . ." I start, but the words have no zing. They die in my throat.

She turns her gaze out the window.

Is she waiting for me?

Or am I waiting for her?

I can feel the weight of life, the hanging question of death. Questions too big to escape envelop us.

"I'll get some tea," I offer. I do, and we hardly speak. But at the end, she gives me another letter. I open it as soon as I get into the car, and it is all I can do not to go back inside afterwards:

As I wrote my last letter to you, I wondered how long it would take for you to come back. I wondered what you'd make of it. Would you find it too much? Would you find me strange or frightening? Why should I mind, I wonder?

Death is not generally a favored topic. People often only speak of it in caricatured or sentimentalized ways, and many avoid those who have suffered as though suffering is contagious. Sometimes, death is simply considered a gateway to life after death—as we have also talked about. But I sense that neither of us are satisfied with that. Still, I don't think our conversations on the topic have been easy for you. I wouldn't have blamed you if you hadn't come back, or for avoiding me because I brought it up again in my letter . . . but I did hope you would return, and I am grateful for it.

You are searching for answers, and I know how that feels. So, despite whatever difficulties arise, our conversations are worthwhile. You are courageous.

Chapter 5

LATE NIGHT VISITS TO the emergency department are not the best part of parenting. And here I am, my youngest son with his jumper soaked in blood after an overzealous leap off the couch, and a subsequent bite through his bottom lip. He leans back against me, eating kernels of corn from the frozen bag that has been used to keep the swelling down. By now he is somewhat settled, but the cut is too deep to leave alone. I hate knowing what is coming; knowing that I will probably have to hold him down while his cut is stitched. I cannot handle this. The blood itself makes my head spin to look at. Why? It is a crimson reminder of mortality; I cannot see it without getting heady. I keep my eyes straight ahead. He is much more relaxed than I am, and he is the injured one. By the end of the episode, my heart has received yet another strike into its depths beyond what I feel I can handle. I am relieved it was not worse, but I go to bed and cry again, exhausted by the pain I have witnessed and the vulnerability that is becoming too real to avoid.

* * *

"So . . . were you a Christian back then?" I ask. We talk at a café today. It is a nice change and a good distraction.

"Oh, I still *am* one, aren't I dear?" she says.

I grin. Who would dare argue? Who would want to?

Right. Me. Yet, who am I to judge? And why does judgment seem so imperative?

Hot chocolates are the order of the day. The relaxed feel of the café with its earthy tones and wide windows is counteracted by the buzz of the customers, jiggling in line for a fix that will not subdue their nerves. We are settled into a quiet corner, away from the hubbub and the constant calls of "Macchiato for Tony!" I don't want people to hear our talk anyhow.

"That book you wrote about," I say, "the one about near-death experiences . . . do you still have it?"

She looks amused. "Do you want to read it?"

"I don't know!" I confessed. "I guess I'm curious."

"Well, truth be told, I threw it out."

"What?!"

She laughs. "Oh, it took a while before I had the confidence to cast it off like that. But I realized such anxiety-riddled questions weren't worth my time."

Looking at her, I can believe it. Something about that quiet dignity surfaces again.

"But . . . did you solve it then?"

Her face is a question.

"I mean, how did you solve the question of life after death?" I timidly venture.

"Solve!" She chortles . . . and her gaze is fixed upon me, as though trying to figure me out.

I swallow and gather my courage. "Thanks for trusting me."

She nods. "You trusted first."

"Did I?" I am surprised, because I sure as heck didn't think that all my anxiety and self-consciousness were an expression of trust; quite the opposite.

"Trust takes courage," she continues, as if gaining an inkling of my surprise. "It's always a risk. A genuine risk."

I nod. Hmmm. This changes things. It changes how I feel about myself.

* * *

We are side by side, driving home.

"You're right," I venture again, "It was hard to read about death. It makes me feel sick to talk about it. Sort of like God."

She smiles and nods.

"There's this odd contradiction in me," I continue. "I'm desperately trying to avoid the big questions—God, death, who I am—but there's an opposite pull of such strength to face them at the same time. I'm caught in the middle."

"Yes, I can see it," she says.

"God is such an odd idea," I continue. "God makes people scared, unhappy, anxious, judgmental, and controlling. But people also say that God makes them nicer and kinder and patient and motivated."

She continues to absorb my thoughts; she is a blank page, filling with my words.

"Would you like another letter?" she asks.

"Yes," I nod. "Yes, please. This almost feels like a mystery and I want to know how it's solved. That's probably not the right way to put it, but even in your letter, you talked about wanting answers, remember? Like finding answers to math problems."

"Yes."

"I think I want that stability too. It means I won't make so many mistakes, because I'll know the answers to things. Then I can predict what's coming and know what to do."

"What mistakes do you make, dear?"

"My whole life is a mistake," I confess.

I get the feeling she doesn't buy it. I know there is no point trying to convince her.

Back home, I help her out of the car, get her walker out of the trunk and unfold it, and help her to the door. I am shocked again by how aged she seems in two years. It reminds me about the lingering question, the loose thread that I have almost forgotten is there. Is she ill? Is she suffering more than she lets on? I must remember to look out for signs, but truthfully, I have been so caught up in our conversations and so selfishly focused on the tumult of my own thought that it has slid from my line of sight. I watch her as she shuffles carefully to the door, struggles to make the small step, and slowly turns to wave goodbye.

There is something about the appearance of old age that tells a lie. Why are we so quick to question another's intelligence? A lazy eye, broken teeth, drooping skin . . . anything vaguely suggestive of poverty, difference or deterioration. We have strong associations with what it means to be sound of mind, functional, intelligent or even reliable. We are always looking out for reliability. Perhaps this includes reliability of thought . . . logic . . . rationality. Rationality means we can understand; when we can understand it is easier to trust. Perhaps at times it serves us well. Perhaps it undercuts us at others. It surely leaves us open for surprise. Surprises are good now and then. Other people are always more than we suspect.

As I stand there thinking these thoughts, her door opens again and she cries out, "I forgot, I forgot!" I am surprised and walk to her.

"What did you forget?" I ask, thinking she has left her purse at the café.

"Your next letter, of course!" she says. "That is, if you'd like it? You said you would, but you may have changed your mind."

"No, no, I'd like it," I say.

"Okay, dear. It's in my handbag. Have a look around in there." I do.

"Thank you," I say, turning to go. As I leave, I awkwardly wrap my left arm around her shoulders and give a quick squeeze before dashing out.

* * *

My son just will not fall asleep tonight, but I need peace and quiet to read this letter. My frustration grows as I lie in bed next to a little boy whose energy is boundless at the most annoying times. There is no sign of sleep. There is also no point fighting it.

"Bub, why don't you hop out of bed and play with your blocks until you feel tired?" I suggest.

That's better. Roll with the punches. My frustration immediately disperses. Good. I turn on the lamp and pull the letter out of my pocket, where it has been stored this whole time, ready to be read as soon as there is space. While the small hurricane is playing, I snuggle up with the letter. It is thick. I am nervous but comfortable. I feel ready to deal with whatever is raised. I read the following.

My friend,

I told you upon our first remeeting a couple of months ago that, "I write." It may have been a strange thing for me to say, especially as a greeting. But I do write, frequently. My favorite thing to write is a letter. I express myself with more clarity and precision when I have time to think, and writing gives space for that. While I enjoy the company of others, I am never sure enough to be really articulate under the circumstances. I don't know if this surprises you. I have grown past minding too much what others think of me; comfort in one's own skin is a benefit of growing older. Yet I am never quite satisfied with my words.

I have not given you a great deal of background on my religious experiences and context. Not quite like you, I grew up in a home of great religious zealotry, but like you, I was most enthusiastic to pursue religion as a young person. As part of family life and ingrained in my developing identity, this perhaps lasted longer for me than it did for you. It was not until my forties after my sister committed suicide that I began to question the effect that my enthusiasm for faith was having upon my life. Upon the whole, I was forced into a crisis where I had to choose between pursuing my previous quests . . . and living a healthy life. By this time, my parents were growing older and my life was more separate to theirs than it had been previously. Their interpretations of my sister's suicide were particularly painful to me, and forced me to face the implications of maintaining their strands of particular religious perspective . . . they talked about God's will as though it was a fate we were powerless against; they spoke of my sister as though she had been possessed by spiritual forces; they blamed their lack of faith for what had happened; they sought every consolation "in God" and God's mercy. Yet they were also softened.

But for me, I could not face where my previous ideas led in the face of this gutting loss—ideas, for example, on the "spiritual" realm, on body and soul, on freedom and fate—when they were pushed to their logical conclusions. I could not simultaneously live with myself and with the idea of a providential, heroic, theistic God before whom I was powerless or surrendered. It became clear to me that my parents' rationalizations did not adequately account for the facts, nor did they enable them to face reality.

Yet who am I to judge? In the face of great pain, we all generate defenses. All I knew at the time was that if I did not change my trajectory, I would be torn apart, and I had too many responsibilities to allow it.

I do not think an experience such as mine is new or unique. It is in fact, ubiquitous. Suffering is an age-old question. Yet what is it that allows us to develop the resiliency to live through and beyond our suffering, in a way that does not also compound it? It seems to me we must be honest enough about ourselves in order to make good choices, and blind enough about ourselves to keep pushing forward.

I grew up in a Pentecostal faith community. Lots of emotion, lots of show, lots of talk about "the Spirit." The truth was always the truth with no questions asked, because the Bible said so. There was a very strong split between the natural and spiritual world, and this often correlated with a strong sense of morality and correct behavior, overseen by authoritarian tones and an implicit but often derecognized penchant for self-flagellation. But at the same time, my family and my church home could be warm, loving, and generous communities—especially when church services (with their fire and brimstone sermons) finally ended. The threads are not so easily untangled. Religion made us what we were; it was a source of both hope and anxiety. It magnified our projected anxieties and purported to provide the cure. Jesus was the answer to everything. Underneath, I believe we were all desperately afraid and scrambling for stability. It was my home, but it was also terrifying. Yet when you live in such a way, you learn to block out what is fearsome and embrace what is reassuring; it is the only normal you know, so you accept the good with the bad, not even conscious that the bad is there—the real problem being that you are certainly not allowed to suspect that it is.

In my forties, the book on life after death was so frightening because, despite the best efforts of the author, she could find no organizing principle or formula based on an individual's religion, life or beliefs to account for their afterlife experience. Some Christians experienced what seemed to be hell, or the edges of it, and those who would never have labelled themselves Christians were filled with light and love! It seemed arbitrary, like an invisible set of criteria that was simply impossible to speculate upon—a rug that could be pulled out from underneath at any moment.

How does one secure one's future or make any decisions before such an unknown, particularly having grown up in a community that existed on the premise of having the precise formula in hand? What did it mean for praying particular prayers, behaving in particular ways, fulfilling particular rites, all of which were meant to generate certain outcomes! A famous question here could be asked: What must I do to be saved? To gain eternal life?

And, what had become of my sister?

All this, in contrast to a very fixed set of procedures that, in the cultural tradition of my church, promised life after death, the very thing apparently needed to create stability and happiness in life here and now. Only it didn't. Because what this book showed me is that this knowledge can never be secured, and the harder you try to bolt it down, the more wildly your freedom presses to escape. Freedom? Yes. Because life is a risk and risk is a wager. It is trust. The fault lines are there, and they run deeper than we can ever gather or understand—and yet, we put one foot in front of the other anyway.

I began reading more widely. I read the work of those who boldly believed that God was just not there; not in the theistic sense anyhow. I had never seriously considered this, but now I had to, and it almost tore me apart.

I cannot tell you the anguish I felt as I lay in bed at night, for the first time genuinely considering what I had never had space to consider—that the God I had always believed in was simply-not-there.

It was as though something deep within me was wretchedly twisted and tearing.

I would start to pray and then realize, "No! No one is there! There is no one to pray to." I felt abandoned. I felt like I was watching God watch me deny his existence. At the same time, I felt similarly to you: How would I know unless I really, genuinely asked? How was it freedom unless I chose amidst genuine possibilities, rather than assuming what I had always chosen to accept? If God was there, wouldn't God value my grinding honesty to my innocent belief? I had to believe that. If God was not like that, why would I want to know such a being? So I decided to wager that God prefers honesty to goodness, or to "religion." And, dear, that is not so far from what the gospel stories tell us after all. It's just that sometimes, one needs a bit of space to see it.

I have risked my life on this wager and it has paid off. I have chosen God by rebelling against God. I have said yes by saying no. It was clear that I didn't, couldn't, and wouldn't trust the invisible God I had grown up with. Funnily enough, I don't think I ever had—I just couldn't realize it until then. And who could trust another who cannot be seen, heard, touched—but who apparently is at the helm of our existence and who many argue affects, causally, our lives?

We learn by our bodies. I have decided that it is an impossibility; we cannot trust God directly. Nor love God, regardless of what people may say. God is loved indirectly. God is trusted indirectly. God is closer than we think. God is close when we think.

This was my revolt against God and it almost cost my life. It certainly cost many friends and, at times, members of my family . . . and it cost almost a lifetime of ideas about myself. Perhaps the deepest, widest cost was my sister. It took that to shake me up.

I stopped forcing myself to trust in a tumultuous idea and began moving forward—just living little by little, embracing life and making the best of it. I knew then that whatever lay beyond was simply unknowable and that I could either cower from it and spend my life in quest of death, or forget it and focus on what was in front of me. To cower meant a swirling abyss ever beneath my feet, draining my energy, fueling anxious behavior, and distracting me from my responsibilities—above all, to my family. So, I let it go and simply moved forward, though not without some drag for several years. I desperately yearned for a cure for all my defects but figured I had better get on with things in the meantime. After a while, I realized that a cure was never going to come.

But I didn't really mind.

Chapter 6

BY THE TIME I get to the end of the letter, my little boy has snuggled up with me and gone to sleep. *What does she mean by rebelling against God?* I wonder, stroking his little back. I am no expert but am pretty sure that hers is one way to end up in the burny place, as far as the common story has it. I think for a while . . . and then do something I have been putting off for too long. I send my mother a text message.

"Hi Mum. Why are you moving so far away?"

I wait. And wait. And I fall into an uneasy sleep.

* * *

While I am washing dishes and hanging washing the next day, I feel angry with her. Not with my mother . . . that's a given . . . but with my little old lady. Of course, I have no right. But letting go of a cure, of an answer . . . I am angry at her for saying what I know in my heart to be true. And at the same time, I realize now that I can't do without her, my companion in this strange journey. I can't help it; I want to visit her every week. It is a moment of stability, anchorage, in the swirl of my life. I am drawn there, as if by a strong current I can hardly resist; as though I have been starved without knowing it and have now found what I didn't know I was looking for.

We have our set day now. It is becoming an institution. The rhythm is almost as much a part of me as walking.

* * *

The next week, I come for the visit armed with another question.

"My impression is," I begin, with the standard cup of peppermint tea in hand, "that you haven't given it up all together. Christianity, I mean." Today, the white dining table is set with a vase of freshly cut flowers from her garden.

"I gave up religion," she replies.

"Yes, but . . . last time we met, you said you were still Christian."

She nods.

"I don't really understand. How can you be Christian if you're not religious? You rebelled against God. You said yes by saying no."

She smiles at my recollections. "Well . . . yes, you're right. I suppose religion makes me think of belief systems and particular behaviors. Or about unity with God, or submission to God."

"Isn't that what Christianity is about?"

"Not to me."

"Then what is it?"

"That is the best question you could ask. Yes, indeed: *what is it*?"

"What is it to *you*?"

"It's about embracing finitude."

"Oh," I say. Then I leap: "What does that mean?"

"It's means accepting that we're humans in vulnerable, limited bodies—yet with great potential to overcome difficulty and limitation, while remaining within it."

She has thought about this a lot. I pick over the words carefully, attempting to detangle them.

She continues, "The thing is, people inspired by Christianity—by the idea of God coming to exist in human form, mingling with humanity, subsumed in every aspect of our lives, even its most vulnerable aspects—have changed the world. There is powerful truth in it."

"Is there?"

"Yes. Every person can be valued, just as they are: human, finite, vulnerable, and complex. Nowadays, we take for granted that human rights exist and that people should be treated as equals. But it hasn't always been this way, and in many ways it still isn't. People have been divided by class, race, gender, culture—and in many ways they still are. But think back to the heart of the Christian message: God experiences what is common to all of us—death. To *all* of us. We're in this together, and even God is immersed in the very hardest, most grueling aspects of human experience. However flawed the expressions of it have been, this idea has changed history."

"But hasn't religion been responsible for a huge amount of violence?" I rejoinder. "What about the crusades? Or the witch-hunts?"

"*People* have been responsible for huge amounts of violence," she says. "But to me, Christian faith is about an idea. And this idea becomes the basis for a stance through all of life."

"Surely Christianity is not the only place that idea is found," I say.

She shrugs. "That doesn't make it less legitimate."

"Then why does it get so muddied? Why has it been so destructive for you and me? Why don't we just leave it behind?"

"Why haven't you left it behind?"

"Well, I tried. It came back to haunt me," I smirk.

"Ha," she smiles. "It's part of us, even more than we know. And it's a matter of taking what's been given and taking responsibility for it ourselves; for shaping it into something good."

"Like, pruning out the bad parts and letting the good parts grow?"

"Yes. And that means finding better ways of understanding and expressing it. And that takes courage."

"That's why it's nice not to have to do it alone," I say, draining the last of my tea. I am not self-conscious, and I mean what I say. We sit in silence and I don't mind it.

"You know what?" I say as a thought strikes.

"What's that?" she inquires.

"I think faith also shows us that love and forgiveness trump bitterness and hate."

"Yes," she nods, "but how so?"

"Because Christ forgave his persecutors. And he accepted all kinds of people. He challenged people who were excluding others.

But it would have been better if he'd just made everyone good all at once, with a click of his fingers."

"Would it?" she questions. "What would it mean?"

I pause and think. "Do you think it's ever worth feeling angry?" I ask. "And do you think there's any point in feeling bitterness or hatred? Do they achieve anything?" We are both pensive.

"Would you like to see my collection of notebooks?" she asks after a while.

"Sure," I reply, surprised. "I'll get your walker."

I do, and we make our way slowly to the bedroom. I feel like an intruder being in here, even though I've seen it before and even though my presence is sanctioned. It feels like I'm seeing too much of her. This feeling doesn't erase my curiosity though; perhaps it reinforces it. I want to ask about the photos and about her husband.

She opens a cupboard. Inside is a giant old suitcase, complete with rusty latches. I see these sorts of things in the op shop and have always been tempted to buy one. And here is hers. She cannot bend down to open it up, so I do. It is filled, positively filled, with notebooks and journals.

"Wow!" I say.

"And that's not all of them!" she laughs. "See if you can find one with a piece of leather string wound round it." I dig around for a while until I find it, while she sits on the bed.

"Here you go." I hand it over and she flicks through as though she knows exactly where she's going.

"Aha!" She finds what she is looking for. Suddenly, she grabs a couple of pages and rips them right out. I startle as the rip cuts into me.

But she looks at me and shrugs, "I don't need them. I carry it all in here," gesturing to her heart. I feel she has ripped it out and given me a piece of it. I don't quite know what to do. I stand there awkwardly.

"Ah, just a moment," she says then. "Do you mind if I write a note to go with it?"

"Go for it," I reply. "Would you like me to get your writing things?"

"Yes please. Just on the side table there is a notepad and pen. I'll sit here and write. Make yourself comfortable."

"I might go and read in the lounge," I say. I am working my way through *A Tale of Two Cities*, but I save it for when I am here. On my way, I rinse out the teacups and pop them on the rack to dry.

Fifteen minutes later, I hear her and her walker shuffling out to meet me. Closing the book with a slight thud, I replace it and go to meet her.

"Here you are, dear," she says, handing me an envelope.

"Thanks," I say. "I'd better head off."

"See you next week," I say, beginning to gather my things. "Oh, wait, I forgot to tell you something!"

"What's that, dear?"

"I . . . I hadn't heard from my parents since the time Dad came over . . . you know, to tell us about moving." She nods. "Well, last week, after I saw you and read your letter, I sent Mum a message. I wanted to know *why* they're moving. You know what she said?"

"What?"

"She said that God had spoken into her heart, telling her it was the right thing to do. Apparently, she thinks she's following where God's leading her! So I replied asking why God was suddenly such a big deal to them, and she basically said I wouldn't understand." My shoelaces become an interesting distraction as the last words leave my mouth.

"Oh."

"Unbelievable," I looked up, contempt swelling. "Who does that? What about me? What about my kids?"

"Indeed."

What more is there to add?

"Okay. Thanks. Well . . . um . . . I'll see you next week then," I say, skittering out.

"Take care, dear," she calls.

"You too."

I reach my car and pull out into the tree-lined street of nicer houses than I've ever lived in. It's a pleasant place, with autumn leaves falling and decorative streetlamps. I drive just round the corner and pull in across from a park.

Her introductory note, written only minutes before, reads:

Dear friend,

Here is a journal excerpt from a time that felt like a pointed crisis in my life. I have never since experienced such utter and complete anxiety, such horrific, paralyzing angst as I did at this point. To look back on, it is hard to believe that these issues were so consuming; it shows how much has changed.

Could I have become who I am now without these experiences? Were they a necessary trauma, like the birth pangs of new life? Or were they self-induced, senseless and needless? Maybe they are neither, simply now a fact of life from which I can learn.

She is poetic. I put aside the clean, new note and pick up the ripped journal pages, decades old. Her handwriting on them is rushed, almost shaky, as if the angst of her body has been transmitted through ink.

I have been reading philosophy. Terrible philosophy . . . terrible because it makes sense. Terrible because as I read it, it brings into question everything I am, and everything I have ever believed. Terrible because I am entertaining the possibility that I agree with it.

I cannot think, I cannot pray; I feel utterly damned, tortured, wretched within the very core of my being. I cannot be myself; I am splitting in two. The part of me that must believe, the part of me that . . .

(Here she had broken off).

Why is it so hard to read such simple words: God is dead . . .??

Why is it so hard to even consider that the unmoved absolute who is the source and authority of my entire life and being, is an illusion?

Why do I feel sick to consider it?

Yet I must consider it; I must test out the thought. But I cannot bear it . . . everything I was, everything I poured myself into, my life, my community, my identity, who others think I am, who I thought I was . . . all of it would be contradicted by experimenting with such a belief.

But am I to be chained to it forever? Don't freedom and growth require exploration and experimentation? How far is too far?

I go to pray, as habit, desiring for God to rescue me from this horrid state, from the anxiety and mental turmoil . . . and yet, I open my lips and am pulled back, as if bound. How dare I call to a God who is not even there? It will solve nothing. I go to call on God, but my unbelief condemns me, checks my inconsistency, with a stupid pinprick of doubt that is sucking in my whole existence . . .

It all shows I do not believe. All this time, I believed I believed. Now I know it is simply true: I never did. I never did. At least now I know it. But what does it mean to "believe"?

And why is it so hard, so traumatic, to consider a perspective different to my own, a perspective quite happily held by many? Why is it too much?

What a stupid contradiction; I am ashamed as though the-God-I-don't-believe-in is watching me ignore him. Yet as I begin to move and change, what I once trusted I now see as unhelpful and false. What was cast as life-giving, I now see as affliction—creating ghettos and swamps which bind thought and reiterate the same sickening monotony, in all its different guises, week after week, month after month, year after year. It makes me sick.

There is no one to get us out of this mess but ourselves. If we consider that God is dead, then the responsibility lies with us; with me. No one can rescue me. And somehow that feels so good, so right—to think, to be a mind, a will, a self. To affirm desire, to intelligently evaluate what I do desire—without fear of reprimand or retribution, without seeking to settle scores or gain points; without having to justify anything.

And now, those I trusted, those who styled themselves as authoritative, I see as empty windbags—just chaff. There is nothing there; no substance. And an odd reversal is occurring: those they demonized, those they painted as outsiders or strugglers, those who resisted religion and stepped away when it became too much; those they looked down upon for their lack of faith, lack of "the truth," lack of "true knowledge" . . . they are not "the bad" ones anymore. They are the ones who are beginning to make sense to me. They are the ones who see all this for what it is: empty.

And I have a mind. I am allowed to step outside my old circles. And as I begin to do so, I begin to fit into a bigger world; it all makes much more sense from here.

Yes. She can write. Driving home after reading this, I am caught in the rhythm of her prose, awash with the tumult of emotion that inevitably accompanies change and growth. Words begin forming in my mind; I am in another world as I wend my way home again. As soon as I walk in the door, I go to my room and sit down. I begin to type and unpredicted words tumble out, saying more than I realized was inside; wisps of consciousness and feeling form into thoughts and into words. I have decided to write too. Isn't that why I initiated this series of visits to begin with? But it is not what I expected it to be. It is not a narrative of her life; it narrates *me*. I type, with increased speed, a few words and a world of relief:

"Idiot!" she screams at herself. "You're a failure! You'll never get there. There's no point!"

This is the tone of her internal soundtrack, day and night. The torment hardly relents. She yearns for rest. Rest from herself, rest from the responsibilities before her.

Day and night she is called on; day and night the children reach out to her. Barely a minute goes by when they do not need something; when they do not need her. And she is dying, strangulating, but she won't call for help. Why won't she call for help?

Because it hurts too much to ask. Because she has asked before and been hit, like a slap in the face. One more slap, and that would be it. She would collapse and disappear. And so, it has hit crisis point. She is trapped. Too afraid to move, yet space constricting ever tighter.

How?

Where?

I have written it down. I consider giving it to her. I know, somehow, she would respond and respond gently. It's funny how you don't hear the tone of your own thinking . . . until it begins to change.

Chapter 7

"Why don't you come along with us?" comes the voice down the phone.

"To church?" I stop in my mental tracks.

My mother has finally phoned. It has been several weeks since she replied to my text message. Apparently moving day is in a month, and I still can't believe it. There is so much I want to scream at her. And this is what she wants to discuss.

"Yes, I really feel that you should come along. You never know which gifts will be imparted."

I pull away and glare at my phone, shaking it angrily. My husband catches my eye from his spot on the couch. Thankfully, he has never had the wool pulled over his eyes by religious people. He laughs at them. It helps give me distance, but I sometimes wonder if he is laughing at me too. However, in this moment, it looks like solidarity.

"Are you there, Hun?"

I am letting forth an enormous, silent scream and still shaking the phone. My kids look up from their show confusedly.

"Hun?" she says again.

"Yes, Mum! I'm here okay! . . . Like you *won't* be in a month!"

"Honey, who are we to argue with the Lord?"

The *Lord*?

"I'm not trying to argue with any *lord*, Mum. I'm arguing with you."

"But it isn't me! It's the . . ."

"*Mum*! Just take responsibility!!! Bloody hell Mum, this is the wrong way round! *You're* the one who's meant to tell *me* to take responsibility for things!"

"And you should! Look, I know this isn't easy, but I'd love if you would come along to church with us just once before we go."

I grit my teeth and am caught like an insect in the tensile lines of a web, pulled one way by my desire to be close to my parents, pulled another by my desire for them to be who I want them to be, and pulled elsewhere again by anger and distance and a sense of disgust.

"Mum, just because you feel something strongly doesn't make it right."

"It does if it's from the Lord."

This is absurd and I can't handle it. She is not hearing a word I am saying. I am not hearing a word of hers either. I remind myself they will be gone in a month. Suddenly, suddenly, I am relieved. Oh my gosh, I am relieved! Something falls away, as though I have slipped out of a painfully constricting dress and it is left lying on the floor beneath me. I can breathe again.

"Mum. I'm not sure if we can come to church with you. Give me time to think about it. But maybe we can all have lunch together before you go."

"Well, alright, have a think about it. I don't know why you're unsure about it, you used to go to church all the time! But anyhow, you can all come back to our place for lunch afterwards."

My parent's house is a hovel and full of junk.

"How about you guys come here this time, Mum?" I say.
"Uhhhh . . ."

She sounds unsure and it is bloody annoying.
"Uhhh . . ."

"Just pray about it, Mum," I say, suddenly giving my husband a wink. I am playing her own game against her. "Then let me know what you think. And I'll let you know about church."

* * *

"What do *you* think?" I ask.

"I don't mind," my husband replies. "It's no big deal to me. I mean, it's not a great use of a quarter of my weekend, and it'll be a total pain with the kids, but it's only a once off and your parents will be gone soon."

I sigh.

"Okay. Thanks. I don't think it affects you like it does me."

"That's 'cos I don't believe any of it!" he smirks.

"And I do?"

"I don't know what you believe. Maybe you're afraid of it," he suggests.

That's annoying.

"I am not," I retort, scrubbing the dining table with unnecessary vigor. "I'm a bit curious to see how I'll go after all these years though. I think a couple of months ago, it would have made me really anxious."

"Why would it make you anxious?" he asks.

I shrug. "I guess because I feel horrendously guilty for not being there more often. In the past I would have felt like I was the target of the preacher's words; like everything was directed straight at me."

"You wouldn't feel that way if you weren't afraid of it. It's a guilty conscience!"

"But what am I guilty of? You don't even believe in God!" I ask in disbelief.

He laughs. "That's the funny thing. Nothing."

I shake my head and I know he's right.

We are going to do it. We are going to church. Partly, I am curious; I am curious about whatever has caught my mother in its orbit. I am curious about how I will handle it all after all these years, and after all the conversations with my little old lady.

* * *

We step into a white, oddly shaped brick building with an open, airy foyer. It is filled with pamphlet stands and has chairs and little tables scattered round the edges. We are greeted with a handshake and a newsletter.

Oh no. The Welcomers.

"Welcome!!" cascades an effusion of bubbles to my right, "Have you been here before?" The fount is a lady with a dark red bob cut and bright cherry lipstick.

I know how this works. I can almost feel their claws sinking into me. They want to know if I'm one of them, they want me to join their ranks, they want people to save, they want my phone number so their pastor can call me and diagnose my spiritual ailments. I shake the feeling off with a shudder.

"Uh no. We're here with my parents," I say. My parents walk in the door behind us.

"Ah, Elsa and Charlie! Welcome!" say Lady Red Hair. The other Welcomer, an older man with white hair slicked back and shiny teeth, follows close behind. They embrace my parents and share more *bless you's* than a sneezy hay fever fit might evoke.

"And these are your children, then? How *wonderful* to have them sharing with us this morning!"

"Yes, yes," gushes my mother. "This is my daughter, my son-in-law, and my little grandchildren!"

Lady Red Hair (whose nametag says *Lola*) goes to pinch my son's cheek and he shies away.

"Sorry," I say automatically, "he's a bit shy." Then I kick myself for apologizing, knowing I wouldn't want her pinching my face either.

Having survived the greetings, we walk into the auditorium. In stark contrast to the foyer, it has no windows; its walls are painted black. What it does have is a bright, well-lit stage, full of flashy instruments and neon lights.

It looks like we've just stepped into a nightclub. Maybe this is why my parents like it. We look around, amusedly.

"Come on, sit with us!" cries Mum, beckoning towards the front.

"Uh, Mum, I think the back is better for the kids," I suggest hurriedly.

Dad looks a little apologetic. He never was one for the lime-light, so I'm a little curious about this whole scenario.

Gosh, it is so long since I've been to church, but it all comes back so quickly as we take our seats up the back (to Mum's annoyance) and I see the musicians and a worship leader walk up the steps to the stage. The guy front and center throws on his guitar and starts strumming and humming, "Mmmmm."

I set up the kids with their coloring books on the floor, stand up, and try to ignore the sound—until my husband catches my glance and makes a mock "Mmmmm" face. It would be hilarious if it wasn't so real.

"Thanks for coming into the house of the Lord this morning," says guitar-man, "Mmmmmm."

Too much reverb. Too much holy strumming.

"It's time for us to lift up our voices in worship," he continues in his singsong way. "Let's bring before the Lord a sacrifice of praise."

My husband leans over. "Did you understand a word of that?"

I grit my teeth and nod. "It's bringing back memories," I say.

It was a sure sign of my faulty faith that I'd married a non-Christian, that was for certain. Mum didn't mind at the time; I of course felt the accompanying guilt, knowing what my Christian duties really were, and how far this placed me down the holiness ladder. I wonder to myself what Mum thinks now. Sneaking a gaze at her, my jaw drops. Her arms are raised up in the air, her face is turned heavenward, and she is joining in the *Mmmmms* that seem intended to crank up the atmosphere before the first song begins. I think back to my old lady's letter and something clicks into place.

The guy up the front begins praying and swaying for good measure.

"Lord, we thank you. We thank you. We bring ourselves before you this morning, knowing that this is the best and only place to be . . . at your feet."

Geez, what about Dad? Is he caught up in this too?

He is standing still, not so dramatic as my mother, but eyes definitely closed. He is into it. Somehow, this is more shocking than

Mum's participation. Dad has never been particularly helpful, but at least he is a counterweight to Mum; he has less of a temper and keeps her a bit grounded. Did they take me to church as a kid to try and gain the character they didn't have? But now, have they found it themselves?

"Holy Spirit, we welcome you. We welcome you," continues guitar-man, and the flashback begins:

I have made the choice. I will follow in the footsteps of those before me and pass through the waters of baptism, dying to my old life (I am fifteen) and rising to the new. It is a beautiful day; we are at the lake. Wide waters, open horizons, space, and fresh air. I am ready for a new beginning. It is the day of my salvation.

We wade out into the gently lapping water; it rises to our waists. I kneel down. There are familiar hands on my shoulders; the moment comes . . .

"We baptize you in the name of . . ."

The Father and the Son . . . I think, following the words they speak as I am submerged beneath the waves. But then—I can't help myself—I veer entirely off track:

But not the Holy Spirit!! I think as I wince.

I have said *no* as I sink down beneath the waves, only to rise up moments later, baptized . . . but secretly only two-thirds saved.

It could almost be a comedy . . . if it wasn't about heaven and hell and all that.

"Jesus, Jesus!" I snap back to where I am in the auditorium as the singing begins in earnest. It is all about loving Jesus and worshipping him and being washed clean. I am certainly too soiled for that, and perhaps I prefer it that way. I feign hearing my daughter call out to me and join her on the ground to help her with coloring, relieved to have invented an excuse to withdraw. While we color, I tune out from the song and my mind wanders back . . .

Gathered in the room, guitars are strumming and the piano is plonking, with the rhythm slightly out of kilter; united voices are led by those not quite in tune. This routine is repeated week in, week out, and we are always trying to find something to make this time more and more special: the ultimate and absolute. Energy is hyped, emotions corralled. I hate when they talk about the Holy Spirit, invite the Holy Spirit, act weirdly and wait . . . wait . . . for what? Some expression of "power," some affirmation of a presence? It sounds like a strange cult, but it is so normal. Those out there just don't understand, they don't believe, and they can't access the resources that we can.

And I switch back and here we are; I am an adult now, coloring with my children. Again, the music swells and the leader's voice is growing louder, more demanding, more insistent . . .

And here I am, eleven years old with sweaty palms, head spinning dizzy, gut churning . . . I can't breathe, I hate it, I have to get out. But oh, *does it make me a bad Christian*? What is wrong with me? Why don't I like it?

It feels like an invasion; I don't want anything I can't see or know *coming inside me*! It sounds like being possessed! I am terrified of being powerless. What if *it* makes me do something I don't want to do? What if I am humiliated?

And yet, according to some, I'm not a proper Christian without it. I have to say yes when I want to say no, when I want to run screaming in the opposite direction to be left on my own, left alone . . . *just give me a book, leave me be . . . I want to be anywhere but here!*

Yet I also want to be included. I want to please my parents, my leaders, my church friends. And I want to go to heaven. Or more to the point, I don't want to go to hell. I am caught in a terrible bind, knowing my salvation is imperative and hating it . . .

Two songs have been sung to a climax which has descended down the other side, and I wonder what it was all for, all this whipping into a frenzy. Is there any material result? A woman in drapey beads and a flowing floral outfit gets up, Bible in hand.

"It's time for us to read from the word of God," she says. "If you've got your Bible with you," (and here is an automatic pang of guilt), "please turn to first Corinthians, chapter thirteen."

The reading is about love. It is about love being patient and kind, not rude or proud. It makes me think of my little old lady, who never barges in. These words don't sound so bad and I wonder where it all goes wrong. Were those Welcomers trying to be loving? Is it love that my Mum is so hungrily seeking?

It suddenly seems so sad. Are all these people here hungry? Just as hungry as me?

As the musicians begin to play again, I move from my daughter's coloring book to my son's blocks, building a tower with him. As the worship leader introduces a slow, hymnal melody, I remember that fateful day when I read the scriptural verses about the unforgivable sin: the rejection of the Holy Spirit. Gosh, I hadn't realized that the rejection of the Holy Spirit was the unforgiveable sin! Didn't that discovery awaken terror in my heart! Me, this poor, pathetic scaredy-cat, now had a whole new dimension of horror added to my fear . . . this was going to cut me off forever! It was the barrier between me and salvation. I didn't like the Holy Spirit. I wanted to say no. But I had to say yes. I remember the contortions it had brought forth as I'd remembered my baptismal assertion—*But not the Holy Spirit!*—and my anguished fear that I was damned and condemned.

As I build block towers and watch guitar-man from the corner of my eye, observing in a manner more disconnected than ever before and thinking back to my great moment of heresy . . . I suddenly laugh. I have rebelled against God. I have been an insurrectionist too! All this time, I have been one. And now, I am not afraid of it. In fact, I feel rather pleased.

Then I remember that there is still the sermon to get through. But it is okay. I have things to do and things to think. My recognition has dissolved my fear, because I am not alone. I can't wait to tell my little old lady.

* * *

Lunch is a moderately painful affair, partly because it is always complicated to be with my parents, partly because my mother insists on commenting on every aspect of our homemaking, and partly because this will be one of the last occasions we will share with them before they go. Of course, it is also painful because my mother insists on saying a protracted grace and discussing the sermon and extracting from us our general experience of the church service. It is hard not to hear the anxiety in her voice, but I am beginning to develop the emotional maturity to recognize it, and not to bat it away too violently. It is a hard line to toe. I decide that in this scenario, it is more important to be kind and keep the peace than it is to honestly confront her with my own stance. After all, I can hold my position without being threatened by hers, without needing her imprimatur, and without intruding into her space. This is new for me. And after all that, the kids are a good distraction.

My parents leave and I agree to come and help with the packing and cleaning—which I will do in small, manageable doses. It is so wrong, but as they walk out the door, I realize again that I am so relieved they are going . . . for all that it still hurts.

Chapter 8

SHE HAS A WHEELCHAIR for longer distances, and today I am wheeling her to the park around the corner from her home. It is a balmy spring day with a breeze brushing past like a kiss. It is strange to be out here, doing this. So unforeseen. Even more surprising to have found a friend with whom I can bare my soul.

At the park, we find a shady spot and I park her, sitting down on the grass myself. We sit for a while, watching, thinking, being. I tell her about the church service, and I tell her how deep down, all this time, I have been enacting my own version of rebellion. I used to be ashamed of it; now it is special, because we share it. And then I have a point of doctrinal clarification to discuss with her.

"Do you believe in the resurrection?" I ask.

She smiles and sits and thinks, and I plait long pieces of grass.

"I believe in *resurrection*," she says finally and firmly, "and I wouldn't be here if I didn't."

Imbued with meaning more than mine, her resolute words leave a lingering wake.

"What is resurrection?" she finally continues. "What is it about?"

"Life overcoming death?" I suggest. "Hope overcoming fear?" I am getting better at thinking beyond the clichéd, flat, doctrinal explanations I grew up with. Instead of nails in a coffin, I begin to think windows into new life.

"Yes, absolutely," she nods, and continues. "We have moments in our lives of humiliation and shame, where we are misunderstood and mistreated by others, where we seem utterly to have failed. They are horrible times; we realize we are not at all who we thought we were; the gap between who we think we are and what is happening seems too deep ever to reconcile. To stare into this abyss is vertigo, being overwhelmed with the danger of falling in." She sighs, feeling the weight of her words. "And what does resurrection mean? It means that despite all this, despite this death of what we thought we were and who we hoped to be, we *keep on going*. We emerge on the other side. When there is no reason to continue, no justification for our existence, no guarantee of our having accomplished anything we hoped for, we press on and we keep trying. We just keep trying, for no good reason—just because we can and because life is here to be lived."

I have an unexpected moment of clarity. "I keep trying to earn life. But maybe I could stop asking whether I deserve it, and just agree to take it—simply because it's there."

"Yes, exactly that," she nods. This is a new aperture into existence.

"And maybe," I continue, "maybe resurrection means that all those questions of being worthy or earning the good things in our lives, or deserving bad things, will fall away—because they don't matter anymore." I pause. "Which probably leaves a whole lot more energy for getting on with things and doing my best."

"That has been my experience," she agrees.

Ha. This feels like revelation, a moment breaking gently but surely into my existence like sunshine into a darkened room. I want to grasp the sunshine, take hold of it, make it my own . . . but of course, I can't. It is a fragile and momentary gift, yet one whose goodness I absorb.

"I have one more question," I add.

"I hope you have loads more than that," she replies, as the corners of her mouth crinkle up.

"Do you think Jesus knew he'd failed?"

* * *

As we walk back home, I tell her my new secret. I tell her about my unexpected feelings of relief that have taken the sting out of my parents' move. She does not judge. She is not shocked. She knows that life is complicated.

Driving home, I feel empowered. I feel that I can choose; that I myself am responsible for my decisions. I don't really know who I am, but I know that I have the capacity to build who I am. I am not subject to fate, even if I am subject to death, and even if there are limits to work within. I am not going to be smote. I can face challenges with grace. I see that life can be received as gift, but that I must also struggle to shape it that way. I do not feel euphoric, because I know I won't ever "arrive." But I do feel delighted to feel comfortable for a moment in the midst of life. To feel comfortable in my own skin is the best feeling I have felt.

I feel strongly the urge to write. I wake up early the next morning, and while the house is still quiet and the sun is elsewhere, I sit and write and write . . . words flowing and tumbling out, as though a vault has been unlocked within me, and everything that was kept numb and locked away is no longer too scary to face. It is okay to be honest with myself; it is okay to feel. She has shown me how. And this locked vault is perhaps my wealth of treasures.

Chapter 9

I AM PAINTING KITCHEN cupboards when the phone rings. The number is unknown and I ignore it. A few moments later, another buzz indicates a voice message.

"Hi . . . it's Kara here. Mum asked me to call you; would you mind calling back when you have a minute?"

Kara . . . I don't know any *Kara's* . . . should I? Then it dawns on me, mid-brushstroke. Ballet . . . Casey's Mum . . . Kara is my little old lady's daughter. For some reason, my heart begins pounding; all the worst possible scenarios pervade me before they've even solidified into proper thoughts and I haven't realized how entwined our lives are until I fear the worst. Hardly able to dial back, I phone Kara and introduce myself, apologizing for missing the call.

"No worries," she says, with a thick voice. "Mum's had some news, and she asked me to phone and let you know."

"Oh . . ." I stutter, "is she okay?"

"Well, as you know, she's been unwell for a couple of years now and is quite frail."

"Mm-hmm," I make out like I know more than I really do, because my friend has never gone into the details of this . . . and why should she have? I don't mind secrets. But I go along with the conversation.

"Um . . . sorry," Kara pauses, and I feel horrid and awkward and as anxious as anything. "Mum's probably only got another week or two to . . . live. A month at most." Kara whispers.

I almost drop the phone. The room spins. No. I cannot comprehend it. I mumble something that attempts at politeness and I am truly grateful for the call, and for having been included in this horrible moment. But I don't know what to do. I know she is old and frail, but I haven't allowed myself to see this coming, and could I really have prepared myself anyhow? And now, oh god, what is my place? Where do I fit? Will I ever see her again? It chokes me.

Of course, I respect her space and will leave her to her family. I have not known her long and her family probably don't know a thing about me . . . certainly not what she means to me, and I'm not sure I could explain it anyhow. But I cannot begin to bear the thought that this is it. I stumble through the rest of the day, feeling angry, feeling guilty, feeling lost.

* * *

After a torturous couple of days, I think about her only every second minute and do my best to get on with things. But it feels like I'm just waiting for the call.

Every time I realize it, I shudder—because I might not even get one. I might not ever know nor hear from them again. It is all too sad and I can barely say more than a few words at a time to my husband and kids for days, who thankfully manage to get on with their lives despite the fact that I have retracted into my shell.

The sky is a sunny blue and the bees buzzing around my newly planted lavender are audible from the front doorway, where I stand. It is four days since Kara's phone call, and it may as well be grey and stormy. I stare outside, looking at my garden, lost in thoughts and feelings and memories. I've barely been further than a meter from my phone for days. And then it rings and I'm already crying . . . but when I answer, it's not Kara . . .

It's her.

"Hello, dear."

I literally drop to my knees in relief and can hardly squeak out, "Hello!"

"How are you?"

I am breathing deep and trying not to cry. I am a master of disguise, so I say, "fine." And then automatically, "How are you?" But I trail off as I realize what I have idiotically just said.

"Oh yes, fine thanks, dear," she says chirpily, though she is perceptibly short of breath. I am surprised and relieved to hear her tone. "You spoke to Kara then?"

"Yes," I reply, having begun to recover myself slightly, "Yes . . . I . . . umm . . . sorry."

"Oh, don't be, dear. It's no surprise for me. I'm sorry I haven't called sooner. I've had many appointments and things to prepare these last couple of days because I've been moved to hospital, and I haven't been very well. Calling you has been on mind when I've been coherent. Of course, I was concerned I might run out of time," she pauses and I catch my breath, for death is caught in the headlights, naked, exposed, "but I made sure to give Kara a message for you . . . just . . . in case that happened."

I am choking again. I can't speak.

"Dear? . . ." Her voice softens with the appellation I have grown to love, and through which I have come to love myself. "I know . . ." She consoles me, when I should be consoling her. "I know this feels abrupt. Endings come too soon."

I burst with tears that are still not enough for these emotions and she is silent, but I know she is there. Right there. Alive. She waits. After a few moments, I can only squeak, "But . . . I'll . . . miss . . . you!"

"I know . . ."

"I thought I'd never see you again!" I say and am lost to everything.

"I'm sorry," her voice is gentle and opens out in me.

"You don't have to be sorry!" I hiccough.

"But I am," she says, with such composure. "I am very sick and I will die soon. But . . . I don't want to leave you. The thought of it is . . . very sad."

I think of her husband and her children and grandchildren and feel so selfish because she is spending time talking with me . . . and what am I? I must think of what is best for her.

"Is this . . . goodbye?" I say, venturing possibly the hardest question of my life so far.

"Oh no, dear!" she replies easily. "Come and see me if you like . . . only if it is convenient, of course . . ." I nearly drop my phone again. Convenient! I'd do anything.

"I'm in hospital now," she says, "but my visiting hours last all day. You're most welcome."

And that is why I love her.

* * *

I want to talk about death with her, but I don't think I should bring it up unless she does. Then again, she has never been afraid of anything I've wanted to discuss. I decide to wait and see, to play it by ear. As I turn into her hospital room, her frame seems so small and fragile on the bed, skin on bones and not much else, yet so much more than that. The contradiction takes my breath away. Her husband sits in a chair by her bed. This is the first time we have met. We shake hands and he seems friendly, but I am thoroughly frightened to think of the impression I am making and I wonder what he thinks of me. He says he is going for a walk, and I am not sure what to do. I tell him there's no need, he can stay, but he is quite adamant about it, and all I can do is accept.

I take a seat by her bed and she turns her head to look at me. I am not afraid of her gaze anymore. I trust it; it is a privilege to be seen by her. As she lies there, breathing seems a mighty effort, and a drip goes into her arm. Her cheeks are hollowed out, and her eyelids seem heavy. I wonder how much of her is still there. What is it that makes her, *her*?

She lies there and looks at me, and I look down to the floor . . . and then I look back at her and shuffle my seat up closer to her bed. I swallow my fear and . . . I take her hand. It is now or never, and I choose beyond fear.

As she looks, she says quietly, "You can ask me anything you want. We've got nothing to lose." I look down because on the contrary, I feel there is everything to lose. "We've talked about so many things," she adds. "Go on."

Does she know? Does she know what's sitting just behind my voice?

"I . . . I . . ."

I can't. But I can't *not*, because it is staring me in the face.

She nods and I gulp, because it is so real.

"I want . . . to sort out what I think. And I want to know what you think. Are you . . . are you . . . afraid?" I say, hardly daring to look up.

She pauses, and responds gently, with a hint of defiance.

"Sometimes. Wildly." She talks slowly, but clearly. "But what is the point of that?" she stops. "Why let fear steal my last days?"

"I don't know." I say. "It seems so scary."

She nods. "We're made to live."

"And you're okay with . . . with not knowing?" I ask.

"What I *do* know is this," she replies. "There are people I love. My life is full of pain and complication now, and it is hard on those I love. My body wants to live, but it also wants to die." She pauses. "You know, at times living life has seemed much more terrifying than dying."

That last part captures me and an inarticulate whisper escapes, because I have known that place too—where life seems harder than death.

She looks at me; I swallow, facing myself squarely now.

"When I was Christian," I begin, "I mean, back then, I didn't think I was afraid to die. I could talk about death and I didn't mind. It was after I left that I felt afraid to look over my shoulder. And . . . there have been times when living has felt like . . . such a burden." I say it as though I am casting it down.

"Yes, of course," she agrees. "We don't choose it, do we? We are just here."

"Is it a bother to talk?" I suddenly ask, remembering myself. "We don't have to talk."

"It's fine, dear," she smiles. "I'll let you know if I'm tired. Besides, I appreciate the chance to . . . discuss things. Sometimes, family is a little too close . . . it hurts them too much."

I nod, and I realize it is my chance to practice what she has modelled to me. I sit, and I hold her hand, and I give her space.

"I want to tell you something," she whispers slowly. "There was a time, after my sister's death, when I wanted to die to escape the pain. I really did, with every fiber in my being. There seemed no other way out or through—except I still believed that death meant facing God, and I was terrified of that too. Living when I wanted to die felt like walking through concrete; the weight of time crushed me, but I was trapped by fear on both sides." She is whispering, pouring each hard-won, feeble breath into weighty words. "You don't help someone who is hurting by chastising them, do you? But I kept chastising myself for my feelings and my fearful thoughts, again and again, more and more harshly, thinking it would make me better, fix me, break me out of my stupor."

She pauses and I freeze, seeing what looks like a tear in her eye. Is it? I can't tell, but it jerks my heart.

She continues, "I was crueler and crueler to myself until I was paralyzed; I could barely move. But . . ." she pauses with the recollection, "there were people relying on me. There were things I wanted to do, even in the midst of pain. I asked myself what I wanted my life to be. My answer was, I wanted it to be *good.*"

She pauses and slowly picks up a cup of water, taking a sip. She puts it down on the little wheeled stand by her bed, adjusting herself in the bed to face me more directly; she looks at me pointedly.

"I had to visualize a future," she continues, "and not only visualize it but decide on it; decide with my mind while my emotions were numbed, numbed because beaten constantly until I could feel no more pain but a crushing weight. I *had* to decide even though I was split in two. And I realized for the first time—and really began to feel—that I didn't want to die after all. In fact, I wanted to live!"

I am nodding, with tears running down my cheeks, because our threads are intertwined, and this is my story too.

"And I *have* lived, and it has been wonderful," she smiles. "I have had to make that choice again and again, but in some ways, it has become easier. So, dear, when you ask me whether I am afraid to die and I say 'wildly,' there is some victory in that. A great deal in fact . . . for it shows how badly, how desperately, I have wanted to *live*. It shows I have been able to own that desire."

Her soliloquy fades.

"By the way dear, keep the Dickens books. They're all for you. Kara knows."

She pauses. "Oh dear, I've been talking at you this whole time!"

I am silent. I grind my teeth; I am breathless, as if hit in the guts. This is simultaneously horrendously difficult and enormously important. I am not equal to it. I need to get out, so I excuse myself and use the bathroom.

When I come back in, I say goodbye to get it over with.

I don't know. I just don't know.

"You can drop in again whenever you like, dear," she says, but I think we both know it is unlikely we will meet again.

"May I give you a hug?" she asks gently, arms slightly extended.

I approach, my heart pounding, and lean down to her tiny frame. I rest my head down next to hers and tuck my face into her neck, drawing close as if I am a tiny child who can hide in her strength.

"Thank you," I whisper.

After what seems like forever and yet no time at all, I pull back and sit down, holding her hand and resting my head on the bed. I want to gather together all she's given me at once, but I can't. It overflows and I'm scrounging but my hands are not enough. I want to hold it all, scoop it all, never let it go.

Suddenly, she gasps with a small cry; she is tense, she is in pain. I hear a caged sob, and she is grasping my hand; my world is crumbling, and my face is turning inside out. Her body writhes and her breathing quickens, and I hold her hand until it passes, paralyzed with fear. She recovers herself partially, but she seems affected, and she is looking straight into my eyes.

"It hurts, but . . . I don't . . . I don't want to die!" she gasps. She is like a small child, vulnerable, fragile, scared. I hold on tight, pat her hand, try to hold tighter . . . but . . .

"Oh!" I gasp, "what hope is there?"

"Hope?" she pauses, looking up at me, holding a whole soul in wide eyes, pained and compelled. "*So* much, dear. There is so much hope for you." A shallow breath. "Do not give up, dear. *Do not give up.* Take life. Grasp it. Don't let anything scare you away."

We are paused, hands clasped, staring fearfully and defiantly at one another. In a moment, her husband returns, and it's back to reality. I am worried he'll think I've been upsetting her, stirring her up. It is time for me to go.

"Goodbye Libby," she says quietly.

"Goodbye Charity," I whisper.

I turn out of the doorway with one final look. And then I leave her to death, with a hundred things still to reconcile in my mind. I have jobs to do, children to collect, a home to manage, plans to make. What an odd juxtaposition are life and death. I know that I will spend my coming weeks in mental conversation with her, planning my next questions and wondering what she's doing, until I realize she is no longer there. I will feel the loss a thousand times. I wonder how my family will treat this grief of mine; will they be understanding and patient? Will I have to hide it from them and bear it myself? But she always saw strength in me, more than I saw in myself. At some point I will find equilibrium again, but not for some time.

What I cannot understand is this: I had thought she had it all worked out. I had thought she had conquered the fear of death, and therefore death itself. She had faced her demons; she had chosen to live. To me, she was all there. But, after all that, I have discovered that part of her that is terrified too. She is as vulnerable as anyone.

And amidst all this, I am proud of her. When I think of her, I see a beautiful collection of loose threads, gathered in the knot that is her, with a core of stability woven together in tiny, colorful lines, none of which ends neatly. I don't think anything ends neatly. There is still the funeral to come, and life beyond that. I have no definitive answers. I have learned a great deal, and now I know this: I refuse to act as though I am always under threat. My life always *is* at stake. That is what life is. But I refuse to make it a crisis. My life is not a catastrophe.

www.ingramcontent.com/pod-product-compliance
Lightning Source LLC
Chambersburg PA
CBHW071315200626
46813CB00015B/2215